Bear in Sunshine
Ours au soleil

Stella Blackstone
Debbie Harter

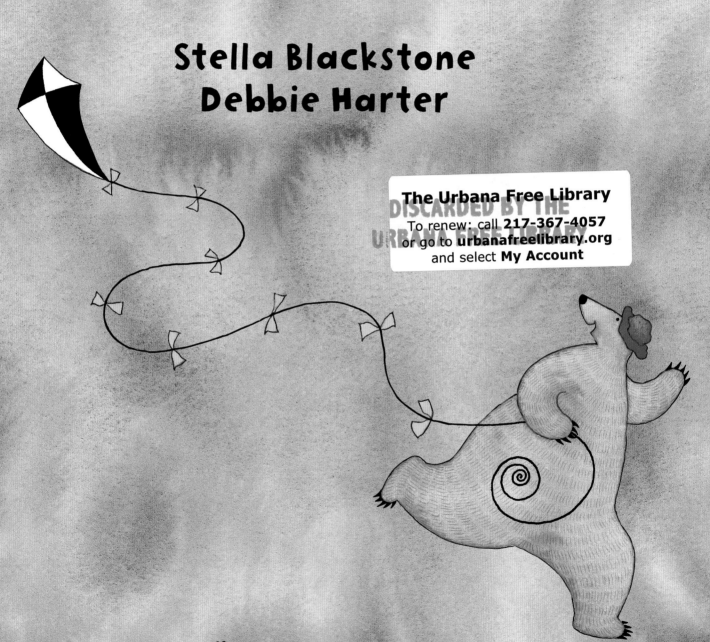

Barefoot Books
Step inside a story

**Bear likes to play
when the sun shines.**

Ours aime jouer sous le soleil.

**Bear likes to sing
when it rains.**

Ours aime chanter
sous la pluie.

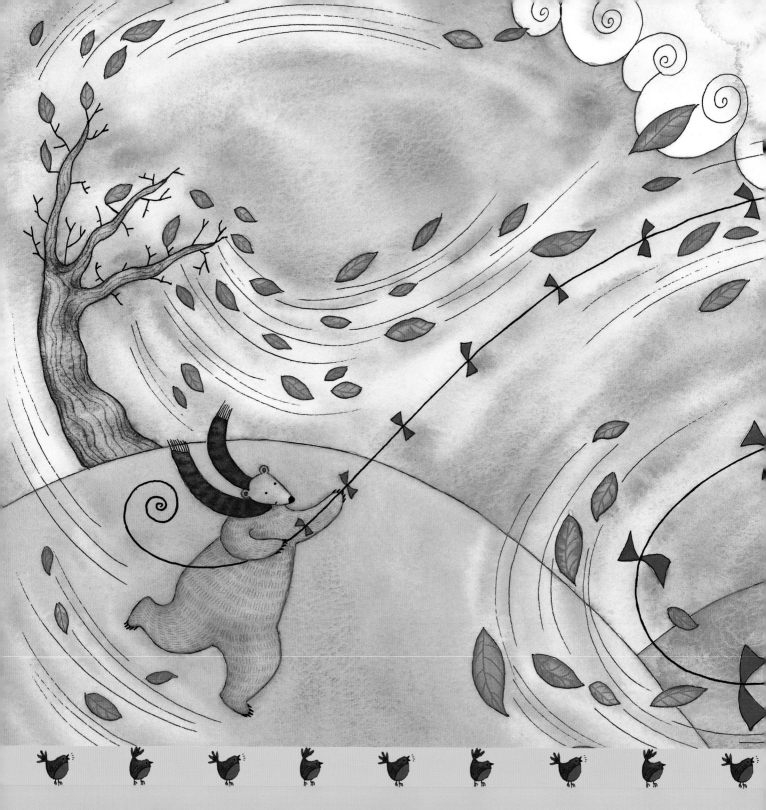

He flies his red kite when it's windy.

Il fait voler son cerf-volant
rouge lorsque souffle le vent.

**When it's icy,
he skates in the lane.**

Quand tout est glacé, il adore patiner.

Bear likes to paint when it's foggy.

Ours aime peindre
dans le brouillard.

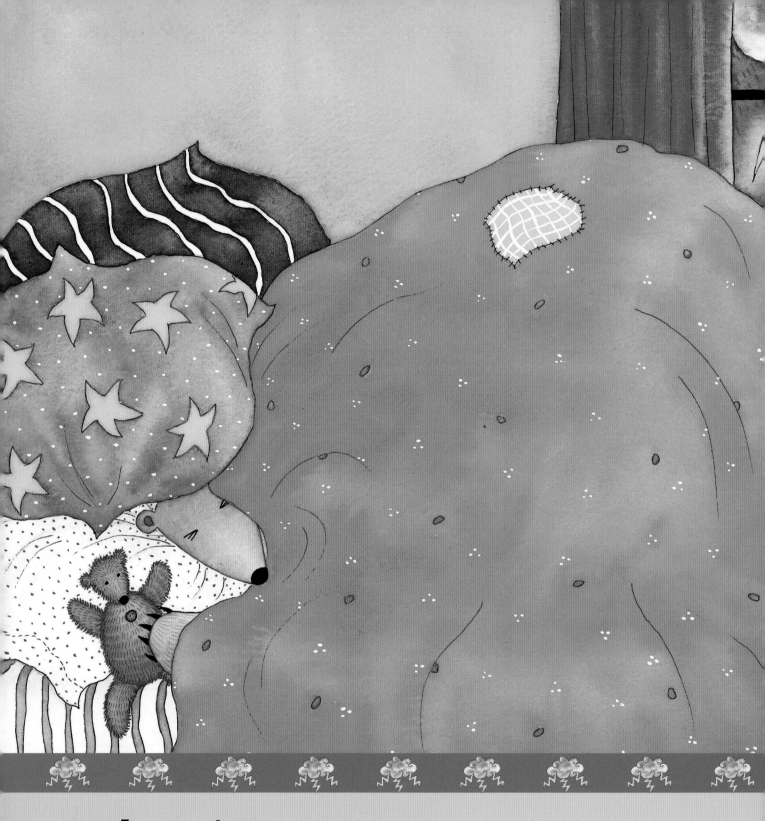

When it's stormy, he hides in his bed.

Quand le ciel est à l'orage,
il se tapit dans son lit.

When it snows, he likes to make snow-bears.

Quand la neige tombe, il fait des ours blancs.

**When the moon shines,
he stands on his head.**

Quand la lune sort briller,
il se met à l'envers.

Whatever the weather,
snow, rain, or sun,

Qu'importe le temps,
neige, pluie ou soleil,

Bear always knows how to have fun!

Ours s'amuse
à merveille !

Spring
Le printemps

Summer
L'été

Autumn
L'automne

Winter
L'hiver

Vocabulary / Vocabulaire

weather – le temps

sun – le soleil

moon – la lune

rain – la pluie

kite – le cerf-volant

wind – le vent

ice – la glace

fog – le brouillard

storm – l'orage

snow – la neige

Barefoot Books
2067 Massachusetts Ave
Cambridge, MA 02140

Barefoot Books
29/30 Fitzroy Square
London, W1T 6LQ

First published in Great Britain by Barefoot Books, Ltd and
in the United States of America by Barefoot Books, Inc in 2001
This bilingual French edition first published in 2017

Translated by Jennifer Couëlle
Reproduction by Bright Arts, Hong Kong
Printed in China on 100% acid-free paper
This book was typeset in Futura and Slappy
The illustrations were prepared in watercolor,
pen and ink, and crayon

ISBN 978-1-78285-331-2

British Cataloguing-in-Publication Data: a catalogue record
for this book is available from the British Library

Library of Congress Cataloging-in-Publication Data
is available upon request

1 3 5 7 9 8 6 4 2